OVER 65 MILLION YEARS AGO

Before the Dinosaurs Died

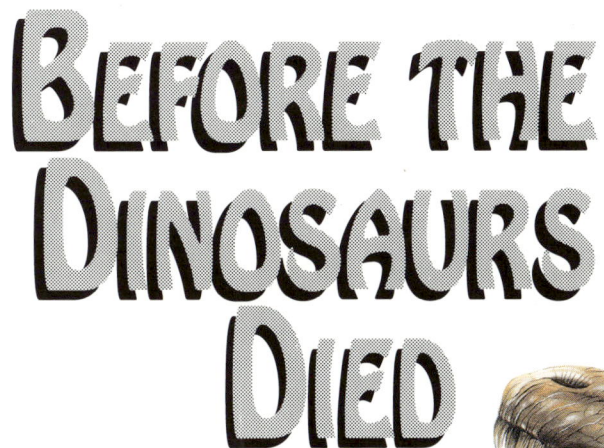

RICHARD T.J. MOODY

ILLUSTRATIONS BY
ALAN MALE

New York

Maxwell Macmillan Canada
Toronto

Maxwell Macmillan International
New York • Oxford • Singapore • Sydney

First American publication 1992 by New Discovery Books, Macmillan Publishing Company, 866 Third Avenue, New York, NY 10022
Maxwell Macmillan Canada Inc., 1200 Eglington Avenue East, Suite 200, Don Mills, Ontario M3C 3N1

Macmillan Publishing Company is part of the Maxwell Communication Group of Companies

First published in Great Britain by Zoe Books Limited, 15 Worthy Lane, Winchester, Hampshire SO23 7AB

A ZOË BOOK

Copyright © 1992 Zoe Books Limited

Devised and produced by
Zoe Books Limited
15 Worthy Lane
Winchester
Hampshire SO23 7AB
England

All rights reserved. No part of this book may be reproduced or transmitted in any form or by any means, electronic or mechanical, including photocopying, recording, or by any information storage and retrieval system, without permission in writing from the publisher.

Printed in Belgium
Design: Pardoe Blacker
Picture research: Sarah Staples
Illustrations: Alan Male

10 9 8 7 6 5 4 3 2 1

Library of Congress Cataloging-in-Publication Data
Moody, Richard T. J.
  Over 65 million years ago: before the dinosaurs died/by Richard T. J. Moody.
    p. cm. — (History detectives)
  Includes index.
  Summary: Describes some of the animals and plants that lived during the Mesozoic Era and speculates about what happened to them.
  ISBN 0-02-767270-0
  1. Dinosaurs — Juvenile literature. [1. Dinosaurs. 2. Prehistoric animals. 3. Paleobotany.] I. Title. II. Series.
QE862.D2M619   1992
560 — dc20   91-44774

Photographic acknowledgments

The publishers wish to acknowledge, with thanks, the following photographic sources:

7 Rida Photo Library/David Bayliss; 11 G.S.F. Picture Library; 14 Rida Photo Library/David Bayliss; 19 Rida Photo Library/P Wellenhoffer; 23 Rida Photo Library/Richard Moody

Contents

A Vanishing World 4

The First Dinosaurs 8

The Ruling Reptiles 12

Upper Jurassic Dinosaurs 16

The Early Cretaceous 20

The Last Dinosaurs 24

Time Line 28

For Further Reading 29

Glossary 30

Index 32

A Vanishing World

The world of the dinosaurs vanished 65 million years ago. Nobody knows exactly what happened, but geologists have discovered many clues to the changes that took place. Great volcanoes were active, throwing clouds of dust upward to darken the sky. For a short period of time, a thick layer of dust covered the world and the temperature fell rapidly to below freezing. The dust and the cold killed many plants and the food sources for many plant-eating animals vanished almost overnight. Without food the plant-eaters would have starved to death.

For a short time the meat-eaters would have feasted on the carcasses of the plant-eaters. Without a fresh supply of meat, however, they too would soon have starved. The disappearance of the dinosaurs and of many other animals and plants took place at the end of the Cretaceous Period. Before that the dinosaurs had ruled our planet for over 150 million years.

Victims of change

Dinosaurs were not the only victims of the changes taking place on earth 65 million years ago. Many other animals and plants living either on land or in the sea also died out. Among these were the ammonites and the reptile families known as the ichthyosaurs, plesiosaurs, and pterosaurs and the giant redwood trees of Europe and Asia. Changes in climate and the splitting of the great landmasses into the different continents affected most forms of life.

The land-dwelling pterosaurs and giant redwood trees suffered badly in the freezing temperatures and in an atmosphere clouded with dust. The pterosaurs were mostly gliders, but the cold atmosphere lacked the warm currents of air that were essential for flight. The redwood trees needed the sun and a clean atmosphere to survive but the cover of dust prevented them from making food.

Sudden changes in the earth's climate may have caused the rapid extinction of many groups of plants and animals, including the dinosaurs and pterosaurs. A thick blanket of volcanic dust would have had the same effect.

Many different types of ammonites lived in the seas during the Cretaceous Period. Their disappearance at the end of that period is as mysterious as that of the dinosaurs. Ammonites were protected by shells that also helped them to swim or float in their search for food. Their food consisted of microscopic creatures floating near the surface of the sea.

A sudden freeze or a blanket of dust killed most of the plants and animals that formed this marine plankton. In turn, this led to the disappearance of the ammonites and other sea-dwelling organisms. The shells of the ammonites and the microscopic creatures settled on the seabed. In time they were buried and became fossils. The fossils are important clues in our understanding of the great changes that took place 65 million years ago. The structure of their shells provides information on their living conditions.

Euhoplites is an example of a Cretaceous ammonite. Many ammonite species flourished in the warm seas of the Mesozoic Era. None survived into the Paleocene Period.

HISTORY DETECTIVE

The bones of dinosaurs are important clues that tell paleontologists how they walked, their build, and their feeding habits.

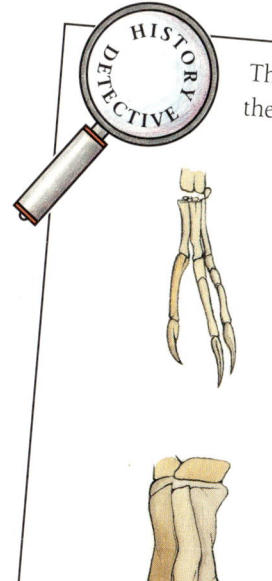

The delicate three-fingered hand of *Ornithomimus* was used to hold and grasp food.

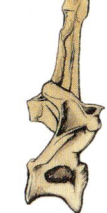

The vertebrae of the sauropod spine supported ligaments and tendons that gave additional strength to the backbone.

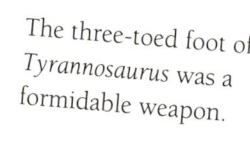

The three-toed foot of *Tyrannosaurus* was a formidable weapon.

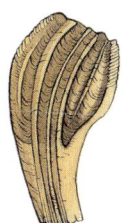

The teeth of *Iguanodon* were leaf-shaped and were used to snip and cut plant material.

THE FIRST DINOSAURS

About 235 million years ago, the first dinosaurs appeared in the southern lands we now know as southern Africa and South America. The climate at that time was hot and dry and the landscape was generally rugged and without much vegetation. The period of time was called the Triassic Period. It began 245 million years ago and lasted just 37 million years.

The Triassic world was populated mainly by reptiles and amphibians. The first, rodentlike mammals appeared at this time, but they were of less importance. Dinosaurs and turtles were new forms of life, with the dinosaurs evolving from the thecodont reptiles during the Early Triassic Period.

By the Late Triassic both two- and four-legged dinosaurs had appeared. In southern Germany, numerous dinosaur skeletons have been discovered, as well as the remains of the first turtles that lived in freshwater ponds.

The largest dinosaur among those found in southern Germany is *Plateosaurus*. *Plateosaurus* was a plant-eater that grew to 19.6 feet (6 meters) in length and weighed 2 to 3 tons. It usually walked on all four legs, but the meat-eating types like *Procompsognathus* and *Halticosaurus* were two-legged. *Procompsognathus* was small and agile and probably roamed in small groups. *Halticosaurus* was a scavenger.

The Triassic world

Sand dunes, streams full of boulders, and salt lakes were typical of the Triassic world. Away from the coast, deserts greater than the Sahara covered vast areas. Mountains were deeply gullied and strewn with boulders. The shallow lakes that developed along the coast often dried up to leave deposits of white salt. Because only a few animals could tolerate such conditions, survival was a constant struggle.

In this dry and rugged landscape, plants were found mostly at the edges of lakes and on the banks of rivers. They looked more like those found in the southern continents today, with species adapted to a warm subtropical climate. Ferns and jointed-stemmed horsetails grew in the wetter areas, and conifers, cycads, and gingkoes grew on the higher ground. The seeds of the gingko or maidenhair tree could survive long, dry spells because they had a protective coat.

monkey puzzle tree

horsetail

gingko

Common plants during the Triassic Period were the gingko, the monkey puzzle tree, and the horsetail. Both the gingko and monkey puzzle tree died out in Europe during the Cenozoic Era.

Outcrops of Triassic rocks are often red or green in color. The red coloring is a clue to the dry climate and the exposure of the rocks to weathering by wind and rain during the Triassic. Few fossils are preserved under these conditions.

The continental landmasses were closely linked during the Triassic. They formed the supercontinent named Pangaea.

Clues to the Triassic climate:
* Rocks weathered to red or alternating red and green.
* Mudcracks on rock surfaces, formed when the lakes and ponds dried up.
* Pits formed by rain. They were preserved in the soft mudstones and sandstones exposed around the lake shorelines.
* The presence of salt layers in rocks, typical of hot coastal lakes found in the Gulf region of the Middle East today.

The Ruling Reptiles

From the Early Triassic up to the end of the Cretaceous, the dinosaurs and their cousins, the crocodiles and pterosaurs, ruled our world. This is why scientists refer to them as the "ruling reptiles." These animals, together with their ancestors, the thecodonts, shared a number of common features. The most important was the presence of a pair of openings behind the eye on each side of their skull.

By the beginning of the Jurassic, the dinosaurs were clearly divided into plant- or meat-eating types. Unlike the crocodiles, however, they were poor swimmers and could not fly like the pterosaurs.

Among the plant-eating dinosaurs of the Lower Jurassic, *Cetiosaurus* grew to over 49 feet (15 meters) in length. It roamed in small groups and the large, two-legged carnivorous dinosaur *Megalosaurus* was its natural enemy. *Dilophosaurus* was a relatively small, two-crested scavenger. It was more agile than *Megalosaurus* and fed on the carcasses of *Cetiosaurus* and the four-legged *Scelidosaurus*. *Scelidosaurus* was protected by a thick, bony skin, but this would have been quite useless if the animal had been attacked by the mighty *Megalosaurus*.

The terrible lizards

In 1841, Richard Owen, then superintendent of the natural history collections at the British Museum in London, grouped the remains of three giant reptile skeletons under the name *Dinosauria*. The name means "terrible lizards." For Owen, the remains of *Iguanodon*, *Megalosaurus*, and *Hylaeosaurus* belonged to a unique group of reptiles that was to stimulate the interest of the general public over the next 150 years.

Dinosaur features

Like reptiles today, dinosaurs were cold-blooded. They laid eggs and had scaly skins. Dinosaur eggs have been found in many places worldwide. They are often found in nests that were cared for by the adult dinosaurs. Mummified dinosaurs have also been discovered in the United States. The preserved carcasses have tough, scaly skins that prevent the loss of body fluids and enable the animal to live in a dry climate, without having to keep the skin moist.

The dinosaurs laid rather elongated eggs. Some dinosaurs built nests and protected their eggs and young from danger.

Many eggs and nests of the early horned dinosaur Protoceratops *have been found in Central Asia. Up to 18 eggs are found in one nest.*

Bones and posture

Dinosaurs were the first reptiles to adopt an upright, or erect, posture. This was achieved by drawing the limbs under the body in contrast to the sprawling position found in lizards. The upright posture, longer limbs, and the development of more efficient muscles gave the dinosaurs advantages over their enemies.

The dinosaurs were often stronger, faster, and more agile, and used their energy to greater effect. The arrangement of the long bones and hip joints also made them more efficient. The hip bones form the pelvic girdle. Two types of girdle are recognized among dinosaurs. The first is known as the "lizard hip," and it is found in saurischian dinosaurs such as *Tyrannosaurus* and *Brachiosaurus*. The "bird hip" girdle is typical of all ornithischian dinosaurs, like *Iguanodon* and *Stegosaurus*.

The hip bones of the dinosaurs are used to divide them into two major groupings: the 3-pronged bird-hipped dinosaurs and the 4-pronged lizard-hipped.

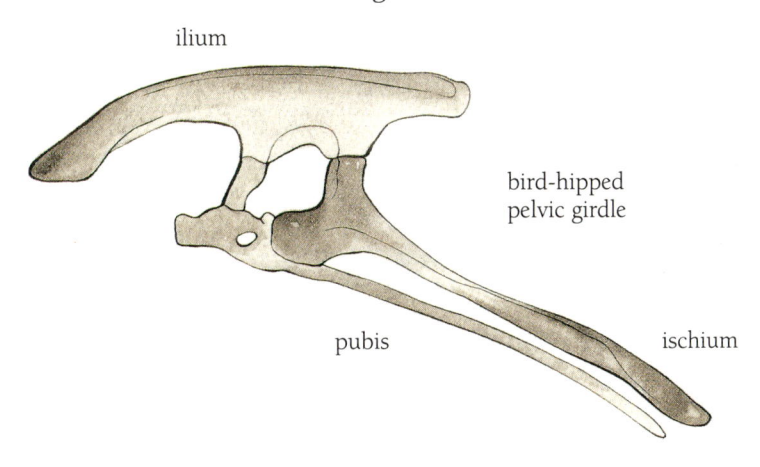

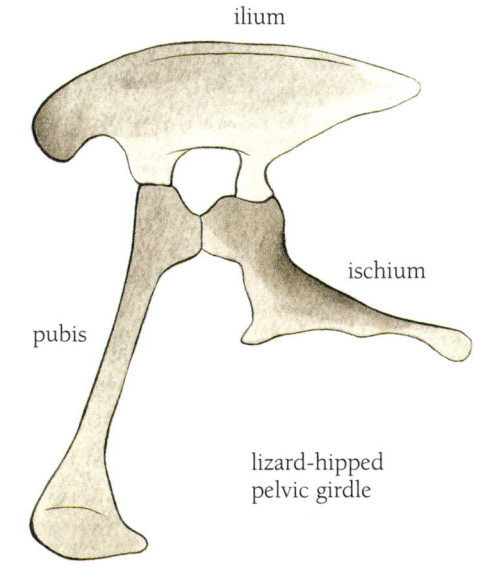

ilium

bird-hipped pelvic girdle

pubis

ischium

ilium

ischium

pubis

lizard-hipped pelvic girdle

Can you discover the answers to the following questions from the clues given on these two pages?

Did dinosaurs lay one or more eggs in their nests?
Were the eggs round or longer than they were round?
How many "prongs" are there to a saurischian hip girdle–3 or 4?
How many prongs are there to the hip girdle of *Iguanodon*–2 or 3?
What did the skin of a dinosaur look like?

15

Upper Jurassic Dinosaurs

Warm seas covered much of our planet during the early part of the Jurassic Period. Around 208 million years ago, however, open plains and thick subtropical forests developed. The deserts of the Triassic had gone and the struggle for survival was less hazardous. New dinosaur families had appeared, with the giant sauropods and stegosaurs as the most important. Both were plant-eaters but the sauropods had longer necks that enabled them to feed from the top branches, while the stegosaurs fed at ground level.

16

East and west

Studies of the Upper Jurassic rocks and fossils of East Africa and the western region of North America reveal remarkable similarities. Both areas had swamplands and the huge sauropod *Brachiosaurus* was common to both. Together with several other forms of sauropod, such as *Dicraeosaurus*, the brachiosaurs ruled the Jurassic world.

As in other dinosaur communities, the plant-eaters, such as the sauropods and plated stegosaurs, were prey to giant meat-eaters. During the Late Jurassic *Allosaurus* and *Megalosaurus* were the most feared meat-eaters, or carnosaurs. Agile scavengers robbed nests or fed on the remains of sauropod carcasses. The sauropods and stegosaurs roamed in small groups whereas the giant meat-eaters hunted alone. The pterosaurs flew over the landscape searching for food.

Sauropods and stegosaurs

Kentrosaurus stegosaur

At first glance the heads of sauropods and stegosaurs look similar, but the length and depth of the skull and the position and variety of the teeth are important clues in their identification.

Stegosaurus stegosaur

Apatosaurus sauropod

Brachiosaurus sauropod

The Jurassic was the period of the giant plant-eaters. Both the sauropods and the stegosaurs fed on soft plant material. The sauropod skull was small. It had a short snout and its nostrils were placed on the top of the skull. Stegosaurs, such as *Stegosaurus* or *Kentrosaurus*, had skulls that were long snouted in comparison to those of sauropods. The front area was beaklike, with small teeth at the back of the jaws.

The sauropods were "lizard hip" dinosaurs with heavy limbs and broad feet, similar to those of a modern elephant. The sauropods *Brachiosaurus*, *Supersaurus*, and *Ultrasaurus* were the largest animals to walk on earth.

Sauropod tracks have been discovered worldwide and consist of deep depressions produced by the slow moving, very heavy creatures. The biggest sauropods stood 59 feet (18 meters) tall, weighed 100 tons, and were over 65.6 feet (20 meters) long.

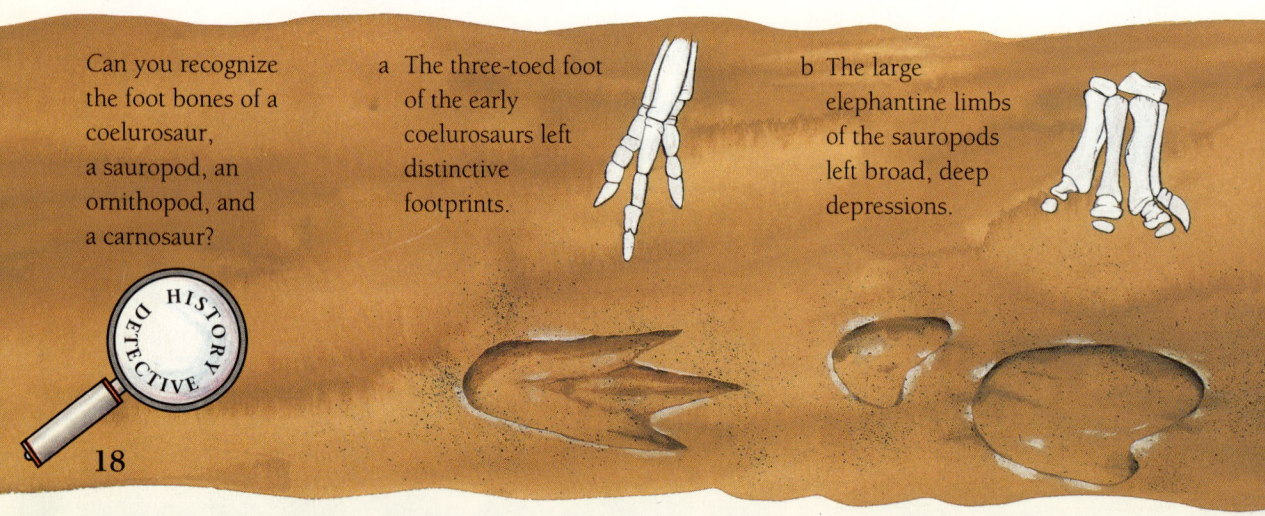

Can you recognize the foot bones of a coelurosaur, a sauropod, an ornithopod, and a carnosaur?

a The three-toed foot of the early coelurosaurs left distinctive footprints.

b The large elephantine limbs of the sauropods left broad, deep depressions.

18

Compsognathus (below) was a small, birdlike dinosaur. Archaeopteryx (right) had a skeleton similar to Compsognathus *but it was feathered.*

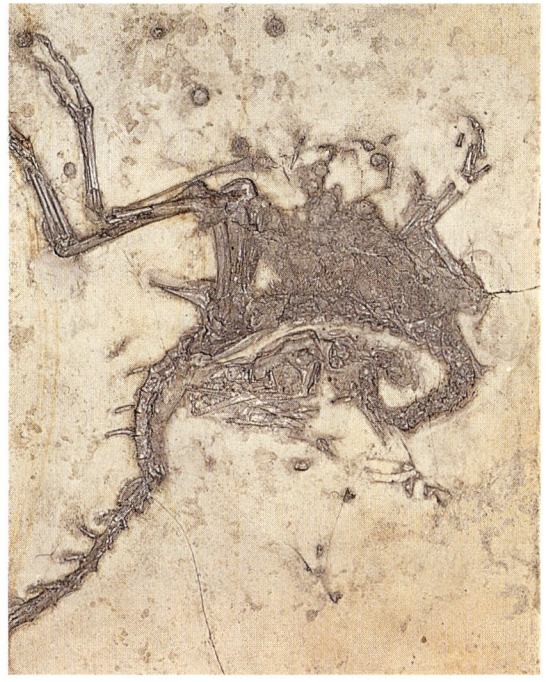

Stegosaurus

Stegosaurus controlled its body temperature by using the large plates on its back as "radiators." Blood could be passed over the plates either to gain or lose heat. Under attack, the only defense of *Stegosaurus* was to lash out with its tail and hope that the plated skin could provide sufficient protection while it made an escape.

First flight

The remains of the first bird *Archaeopteryx* have been found in Upper Jurassic rocks in southern Germany. The skeleton of "ancient feather" or "Archie," as it is sometimes called, was very similar to that of *Compsognathus*, the small scavenging dinosaur from the same locality. Feathered wings and tail suggest that *Archaeopteryx* could fly. It fed on insects and small reptiles that it killed with a bite of its sharp teeth.

c Three-toed footprints, which were broad, even hooflike, were characteristic of the duck-billed dinosaurs.

d *Tyrannosaurus* ran with one foot landing almost directly in front of the other. The foot of this meat-eater had three large toes.

THE EARLY CRETACEOUS

20

The Cretaceous was a period of change. The continents were drifting farther and farther apart, and new seaways were formed across northern Africa and North America. New types of flowering plants such as laurel, poplar, magnolia, and cinnamon appeared. They provided food for a host of insects. New families of dinosaurs replaced the sauropods and stegosaurs in number and importance. Some Jurassic sauropods like *Cetiosaurus* survived because the swampy conditions essential to their existence were available to them throughout Europe, North America, northwest Africa, and Asia. The sauropods existed alongside *Iguanodon* and *Hypsilophodon* in Europe and North America, and with the "sail-back" dinosaur, *Ouranosaurus*, in Africa. All were peaceful plant-eaters.

A new danger?

Until recently it was thought that *Megalosaurus* was the only major meat-eater of the Early Cretaceous. However, the discovery of a *Baryonyx* skeleton revealed the existence of a family of vicious, agile predators. Armed with sharp teeth and a high slashing claw 12 inches (31 centimeters) long, *Baryonyx*, or "super claw," could have put up a formidable defense.

A changing world

The dawn of the Lower Cretaceous took place approximately 146 million years ago. South America and the Australo-Antarctic landmasses were now isolated and Africa was only connected to the northern super-continent by a single land bridge. Because migration between and across continents had become more difficult, reptile and mammal communities became isolated. The major changes in dinosaur history were taking place in the north.

Although the southern landmass had fragmented by the Lower Cretaceous, the northern continent of Laurasia still existed.

Hypsilophodon and *Baryonyx* were examples of advanced Cretaceous dinosaurs. Their home was the northern landmass called Laurasia.

Baryonyx

Hypsilophodon

Super claw

The discovery of *Baryonyx* in the rocks of the Early Cretaceous of southern England in 1983 provided new information on the meat-eating dinosaurs. Scientists now believe that the claw and the sharp teeth arranged in a long snout were adaptations to hook and catch fish, similar to brown bears in North America today.

Long before the discovery of *Baryonyx* in England, a single claw had been found in the desert wastes of Niger in West Africa. It would appear that fish-eating dinosaurs were spread far and wide.

An agile ornithopod

The wet lands of southern England were home to *Hypsilophodon*. It measured about 3.3 feet (1 meter) in length, and the structure of the hind limbs suggests it moved in leaps and bounds, darting sideways to avoid capture.

These models of Megalosaurus *(left) and* Iguanodon *(below) were built by Waterhouse Hawkins in 1854. Today they are displayed at Crystal Palace in Sydenham, England.*

Megalosaurus

Megalosaurus was one of the longest-lived dinosaurs. It first appeared during the Jurassic and may have survived into the Upper Cretaceous, a period of 70 million years. There is little doubt that *Megalosaurus* was succeeded as the dominant meat-eater by *Tyrannosaurus rex*. *Tyrannosaurus* weighed up to 8 tons and was the largest meat-eater ever to have lived. *Megalosaurus* was unable to compete with *Tyrannosaurus rex* as it was less agile and smaller, so it died out.

The changes in dinosaur communities between the Lower and Upper Cretaceous were significant, with *Iguanodon* being replaced by the duck-billed and crested hadrosaurs. These changes were due to competition and the survival of the fittest.

These plants first appeared during the Cretaceous Period, and they can still be found in different parts of the world today. Can you find any of them in your area?

magnolia

poplar

laurel

cinnamon

The Last Dinosaurs

Seventy million years ago, the world was a very different place, different from the one we know today and different from the world that had witnessed the evolution of the first dinosaurs 150 million years earlier in the Triassic. The southern continents had drifted apart and broad plains covered vast areas of North America and Asia. Flowering plants, including the first magnolias and roses, colored the landscape. Dinosaurs were rare in the southern continents but, in the north, herds of horned *Triceratops* and duck-billed species like *Parasaurolophus* roamed the lands. Males and females, young and old, grazed side by side with smaller groups of the heavily armored *Euplocephalus* and *Scolosaurus*.

A great catastrophe

The herds of dinosaurs in North America and Asia were stalked and hunted by huge meat-eaters such as *Tyrannosaurus rex*. The remains of a dinosaur were a source of food for numerous creatures. Hunting and killing was the normal relationship between the meat-eaters and their prey. However, the total amount of dinosaurs killed was small and would never be considered as a cause for extinction.

Many groups of animals and plants vanished at the end of the Late Cretaceous. The mystery of their disappearance remains. Was it gradual or the result of a great explosion in outer space? Perhaps a "global winter" occurred as the result of intense volcanic activity. Darkened skies, freezing temperatures, little food, and a world totally unsuited to animals that enjoyed warmth may have been signs of the end of the dinosaurs.

Hadrosaurs

Duck-billed hadrosaurs first appeared 100 million years ago in Mongolia. Seventy-five million years ago, two distinct groups of duck-billed dinosaurs had evolved. The first were the kritosaurs or flat-headed hadrosaurs. Their faces were narrow with a swelling or hump in front of their eyes. *Kritosaurus* could inflate an area of the snout. If the enlarged beak was brightly colored, it could strike fear into an opponent or an unsuspecting meat-eater. *Corythosaurus* was a crested duck-billed dinosaur. The crest varied in size between young and old, male and female.

The duck-billed dinosaurs were related to the bird-hipped *Iguanodon*. The earliest duck-bill was *Bactrosaurus*, which gave rise to the hump-nosed and crested species of the Upper Cretaceous.

The crested duck-bills are known as saurolophines. *Parasaurolophus* possessed a spectacular tubelike structure. This structure may have allowed the animals to make sounds. The crests were also display features, reflecting the ranks within the herd.

By the Upper Cretaceous Period, the Atlantic Ocean had grown wider, separating the Americas from Africa.

Ceratopsians

The ceratopsians are also called the horn face or frilled dinosaurs. *Psittacosaurus*, the "parrot lizard," was the first. It appeared 110 million years ago in Asia and was the ancestor of *Triceratops*, a bird-hipped dinosaur. *Triceratops* was a very large plant-eater that lived in large herds. The males grew to 23 feet (7 meters) in length and weighed 7 or 8 tons.

Kritosaurus

Corythosaurus

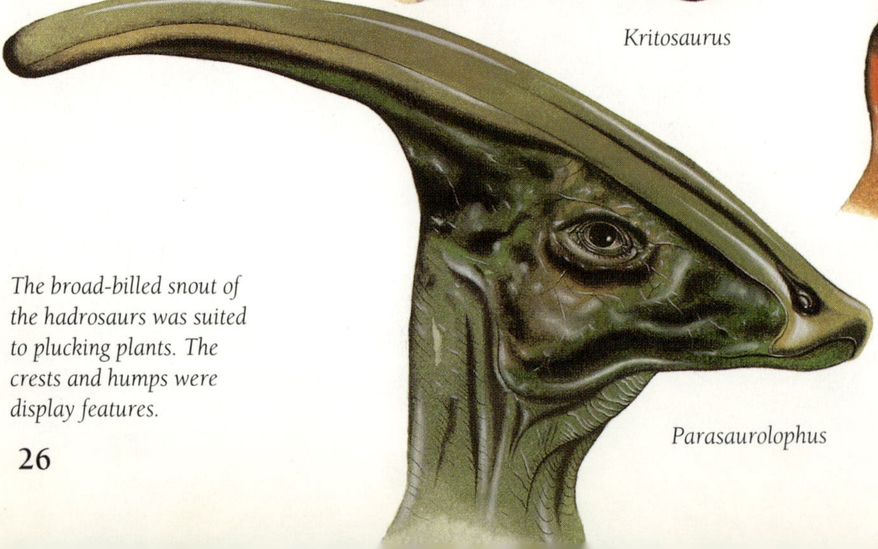

The broad-billed snout of the hadrosaurs was suited to plucking plants. The crests and humps were display features.

Parasaurolophus

26

The importance of armor

The hadrosaurs lacked horns, spikes, or bony plates. They relied on speed and numbers for protection. In contrast, the ceratopsians and the ankylosaurs were heavily armored. The ancestors of the ankylosaurs can be traced back to the Late Jurassic, but it was during the Late Cretaceous that they began to resemble "reptilian tanks." *Scolosaurus* was a squat plant-eater that weighed 3.5 tons. It had flexible body armor that stretched from nose to tail. Short vertical spikes adorned the side of its body and two others grew on the swollen clublike tail. Its armor protected it against attacks by *Tyrannosaurus rex*.

Triceratops *had a huge bony frill over its neck, and three horns on its face. They provided protection against attack.*

Scolosaurus *was a slow moving creature with plated armor from nose to tail. Like most ankylosaurs, it was short-limbed.*

Armored and slow

* Armor was used to protect the neck or the soft underbelly from attacks by a large predator. It may have taken the form of facial horns, bony frills, thick bony plates, nodes, or spines.

* Heavily armored or well-protected dinosaurs were usually four-legged and heavily built – for example, ceratopsians and ankylosaurs.

* Body armor is associated with the slower moving grazers or browsers. An armored "skin" limits movements in most animals, e.g. the tortoise.

Unarmored and agile

* The hadrosaurs and tyrannosaurs lacked armor. Both had powerful back legs. Their skins were scaly but not thickened by bony plates or nodes like the crown reptiles. Both groups lacked spikes or spines.

* The lack of armor, horns, or frills is typical of two-legged dinosaurs. Speed and agility are important to such creatures.

* The hadrosaurs were plant-eaters, while the tyrannosaurs ate meat. Hadrosaurs ran away to avoid attack. The tyrannosaurs relied on speed to hunt.

Time Line

Million years ago

4,600	Earth is formed in space and starts to rotate around the sun	Precambrian
3,500	First signs of life on earth	Era
3,300	First single-celled creatures	

600	First communities	
480	First fishes	
430	First land plants and animals	
400	Ancestors of the ammonites appear	Paleozoic
380	First amphibian	Era
330	Swampland forests over huge areas of the northern landmasses First reptile	
245	Many groups of animals and plants die out	

245	Start of Triassic Period Main plant groups until 100 million years ago: ferns, conifers, cycads, and bennetitaleans	Mesozoic
240	First mammals	Era
235	First dinosaurs, e.g. *Herrerasaurus*	
220	Saurischian and ornithischian dinosaurs are represented in southern and northern hemispheres, e.g. *Plateosaurus* and *Fabrosaurus*	

208	Start of Jurassic period Giant carnosaurs and sauropods, e.g. *Megalosaurus* and *Cetiosaurus*	
165	First bird, *Archaeopteryx*, appears Camptosaurs, relatives of *Iguanodon*, live in Africa and America	
146	Start of Cretaceous Period First known flowering plants	
130	First ankylosaurs appear, e.g. *Ankylosaurus*	
110	First horned dinosaurs appear, e.g. *Psittacosaurus*	
90	First duck-billed dinosaurs evolve, e.g. *Corythosaurus*	
70	Herds of dinosaurs roam northern continents	
65	Death of many groups of animals and plants, including ammonites, pterosaurs, and giant tree species All dinosaurs die out	
65	Paleocene Period lasts approximately 10 million years	Cenozoic Era

For Further Reading

Chenel, Pascale. *The Life and Death of Dinosaurs*. Happauge, New York: Barron 1987.
Crenson, Victoria. *Discovering Dinosaurs: An Up-to-Date Guide Including the Newest Theories*. Los Angeles: Price Stern, 1988.
Knight, David C. *Dinosaurs that Swam and Flew*. Englewood Cliffs, New Jersey: Prentice-Hall, 1985.
Lambert, David. *The Age of Dinosaurs*. New York: Random House, 1987.
Lampton, Christopher. *Mass Extinctions: One Theory of Why the Dinosaurs Vanished*. New York: Franklin Watts, 1986.
Matthews, Rupert. *The Dinosaur Age*. New York: Bookwright, 1989.
Norman, David and Angela Miller. *Dinosaur*. New York: Knopf, 1989.
Stidworthy, John. *The Day of the Dinosaurs*. Morristown, New Jersey: Silver Burdett, 1986.

Glossary

adaptations: changes made by an animal or plant that allow it to thrive within its own environment

ammonite: a mollusk with a chambered shell

amphibian: an animal with a backbone that lays eggs in water. The eggs hatch into tadpoles that have gills and live in the water. The adults have lungs and can live on land. Frogs and toads are amphibians.

ancestor: a relative who lived and died a long time ago

ankylosaurs: heavily armored four-legged ornithischian dinosaurs, e.g. *Ankylosaurus* and *Scolosaurus*

brachiosaurs: gigantic, four-legged, long-necked sauropods from the Jurassic Period, e.g. *Brachiosaurus*

carnivorous: describes a meat-eating animal

carnosaurs: large, meat-eating, lizard-hipped dinosaurs, e.g. *Tyrannosaurus rex*

catastrophe: a sudden disastrous happening that may cause death and destruction

ceratopsians: horned dinosaurs of the Cretaceous Period, e.g. *Triceratops*

coelurosaurs: small to medium-size, lizard-hipped dinosaurs, e.g. *Compsognathus*. They were two-legged scavengers.

cold-blooded: describes animals that do not generate heat from their food. Reptiles are cold-blooded.

conifer: an important group of trees that first appeared at the end of the Permian Period. They include firs and pines.

crest: a bony plate or hollow tubelike structure found in duck-billed dinosaurs, e.g. *Parasaurolophus*

Cretaceous: the last of three periods that are included in the Mesozoic Era. The Cretaceous lasted from 146 to 65 million years ago.

cycads: an important group of plants that grew during the Jurassic Period. They had long simple leaves set in a crownlike setting.

deposits: describes rock materials left by wind or ice

dinosaurs: a group of reptiles with two openings in the wall of the skull behind the eye socket

display features: frills of skin, crests, or highly colored skin patterns that were used to startle or frighten an enemy, or impress a member of the same herd

dominant: describes the success of one group of animals over another or of a large male dinosaur over young challengers for the leadership of a herd

dunes: hills of sand built up by the action of the wind

era: a geological time unit made up of periods. The Mesozoic Era includes the Triassic, Jurassic, and Cretaceous periods.

erect: describes an upright position

extinct: describes animals and plants that have died out leaving no known representatives

30

fossils: the remains of animals and plants that lived millions of years ago

geologist: a scientist who studies rocks and fossils

hadrosaurs: duck-billed or crested dinosaurs with a birdhip, e.g. *Kritosaurus*

horsetails: plants with jointed stems and thin pointed leaves arranged in small circles around the stem

ichthyosaurs: streamlined fish-eating reptiles of the Mesozoic Era, often known as "fish lizards"

Jurassic: the second or middle of the three periods of the Mesozoic Era. It lasted from 208 to 146 million years ago.

mammals: warm-blooded animals that give birth to live young

Mesozoic: the so-called age of "middle life" that lasted from 245 to 65 million years ago

migration: the movement of animals from one region to another to find new feeding grounds. It is often associated with a change of season.

nodes: raised and rounded bony structures on a dinosaur skin

ornithischian: bird-hipped dinosaurs, e.g. *Iguanodon* or *Camptosaurus*

paleontologist: a geologist who studies fossilized plants and animals

plankton: microscopic organisms that float near the surface of the water

predator: an animal that hunts and kills its prey. *Tyrannosaurus rex* and the lion are both predators.

pterosaurs: flying reptiles that evolved from the same ancestors as the dinosaurs

reptile: an animal with a dry, scaly skin that lays eggs protected by a shell. Because reptiles cannot make their own body heat, they are cold-blooded. Dinosaurs, pterosaurs, crocodiles, and turtles are all reptiles.

saurischian: lizard-hipped dinosaurs, e.g. *Brachiosaurus* and *Tyrannosaurus*

saurolophines: a group of duck-billed dinosaurs that developed a distinct crest on the back of the head

sauropods: lizard-hipped dinosaurs, e.g. *Brachiosaurus*. They had broad-toed feet, similar to those of an elephant.

scavengers: animals that "clean up" after larger predators have eaten their fill

scientists: men and women who observe, measure, and record data; conduct experiments and describe the results. Chemists, physicists, and geologists are scientists.

squat: describes a heavily built, low-standing creature, e.g. *Ankylosaurus*

stegosaurs: four-legged, bird-hipped dinosaurs with plated or spiny backs, e.g. *Stegosaurus*

structure: the way something is made or built up

subtropical: the climate found in regions around the tropics of Cancer and Capricorn where the sun is immediately overhead in the midsummer months

thecodonts: the tooth-in-socket reptiles. Thecodonts were the ancestors of dinosaurs, crocodiles, and pterosaurs.

Triassic: the first period of the Mesozoic Era, which lasted from 245 to 208 million years ago

tyrannosaurs: a group of gigantic, meat-eating lizard-hipped dinosaurs from the Upper Cretaceous Period

INDEX

Africa 8, 17, 20, 21, 22, 26
Allosaurus 17
ammonites 6, 7
amphibians 8
ankylosaurs 27
Archaeopteryx 19
Asia 6, 14, 21, 24, 25, 26

Bactrosaurus 26
Baryonyx 21, 22
bones 7, 15
  bird-hipped dinosaurs 15, 26
  lizard-hipped dinosaurs 15, 18
brachiosaurs 17
Brachiosaurus 15, 17, 18

ceratopsians 26, 27
Cetiosaurus 13, 21
climate 6, 8, 11
Compsognathus 19
Corythosaurus 26
Cretaceous Period 5, 7, 12, 20, 21, 22, 23, 25, 26, 27
crocodiles 12

Dicraeosaurus 17
Dilophosaurus 13
duck-billed dinosaurs 19, 23, 24, 26
dust 4, 6, 7

eggs 14
Euplocephalus 24
Europe 6, 21

fish-eating dinosaurs 22
fossils 7, 11, 17

hadrosaurs 23, 26, 27
Halticosaurus 9
Hylaeosaurus 14
Hypsilophodon 21, 22

ichthyosaurs 6
Iguanodon 7, 14, 15, 21, 23, 26
insects 19, 20

Jurassic Period 12, 13, 16, 17, 18, 19, 23, 27

Kentrosaurus 18
kritosaurs 26
Kritosaurus 26

Laurasia 22

meat-eating dinosaurs 5, 9, 12, 13, 17, 19, 21, 22, 23, 25, 26, 27
Megalosaurus 13, 14, 17, 21, 23
Mesozoic Era 7

North America 14, 17, 20, 21, 22, 24, 25

Ornithomimus 7
Ouranosaurus 21
Owen, Richard 14

Paleocene Period 7
Pangaea 11

Parasaurolophus 24, 26
plant-eating dinosaurs 4, 5, 9, 12, 13, 16, 17, 18, 21, 26, 27
plants 4, 5, 6, 7, 8, 10, 18, 20, 23, 24, 25, 26
Plateosaurus 9
plesiosaurs 6
Procompsognathus 9
Protoceratops 14
Psittacosaurus 26
pterosaurs 6, 12, 17

reptiles 6, 8, 14, 15, 19, 22
rocks 11, 17, 19, 22

saurolophines 26
sauropods 7, 16, 17, 18, 20, 21
scavengers 9, 13, 17, 19
Scelidosaurus 13
Scolosaurus 24, 27
South America 8, 22
stegosaurs 16, 17, 18, 20
Stegosaurus 15, 18, 19
Supersaurus 18

thecodonts 8, 12
trees 6, 10, 20
Triassic Period 8, 9, 10, 11, 12, 24
Triceratops 24, 26, 27
turtles 8, 9
Tyrannosaurus 7, 15, 19, 23, 25, 27

volcanoes 4, 6, 25